© Ludorum plc 2009

First published by Parragon in 2010

Parragon
Queen Street House
4 Queen Street
Bath BA1 1HE, UK

www.chuggington.com

© Ludorum plc 2009

ISBN 978-1-4454-1179-8

Printed in China

BRAKING BREWSTER

Based on the episode "Braking Brewster",
written by Sarah Ball.

Bath · New York · Singapore · Hong Kong · Cologne · Delhi · Melbourne

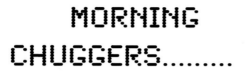

MORNING
CHUGGERS.........

One morning, Vee had an
exciting job for Brewster
and Wilson.

"It's training time!" said
Wilson, excitedly.

Brewster hoped they would
be back in time to practise
his new moves.

In the loading yard, Dunbar gave Brewster and Wilson hopper cars for training. He showed them what to do when they had a heavy load. "Doors...drop... load. Got it," said Brewster, confidently.

**DOORS...
DROP...
LOAD!**

Wilson found it really hard at first – but he kept trying. Then he did it!

"WAHAY"

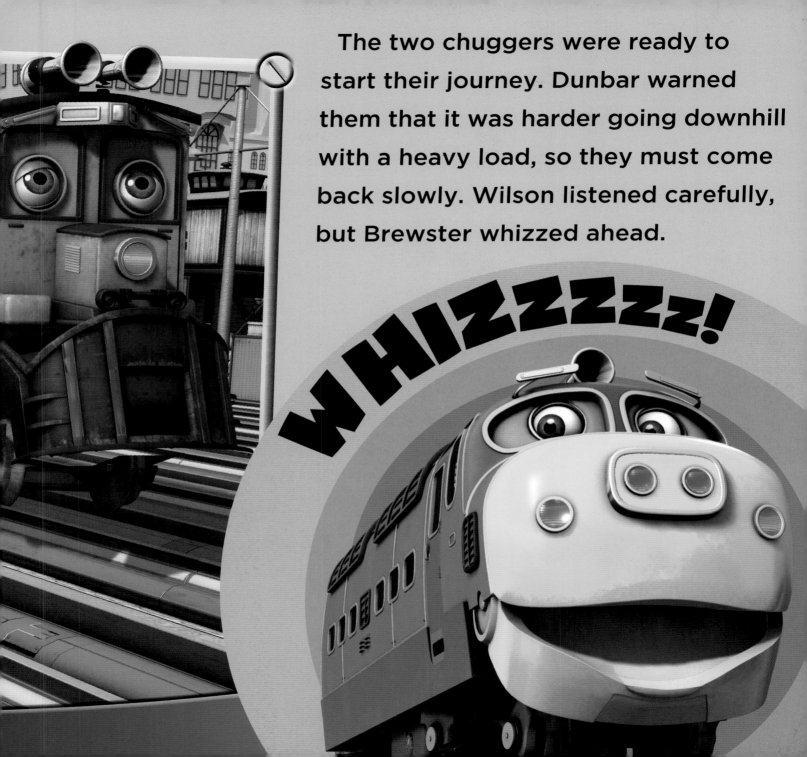

The two chuggers were ready to start their journey. Dunbar warned them that it was harder going downhill with a heavy load, so they must come back slowly. Wilson listened carefully, but Brewster whizzed ahead.

WHIZZZZz!

Vee told the chuggers to go to the mountain quarry to collect stone. They were to take the left tunnel at the mountain.

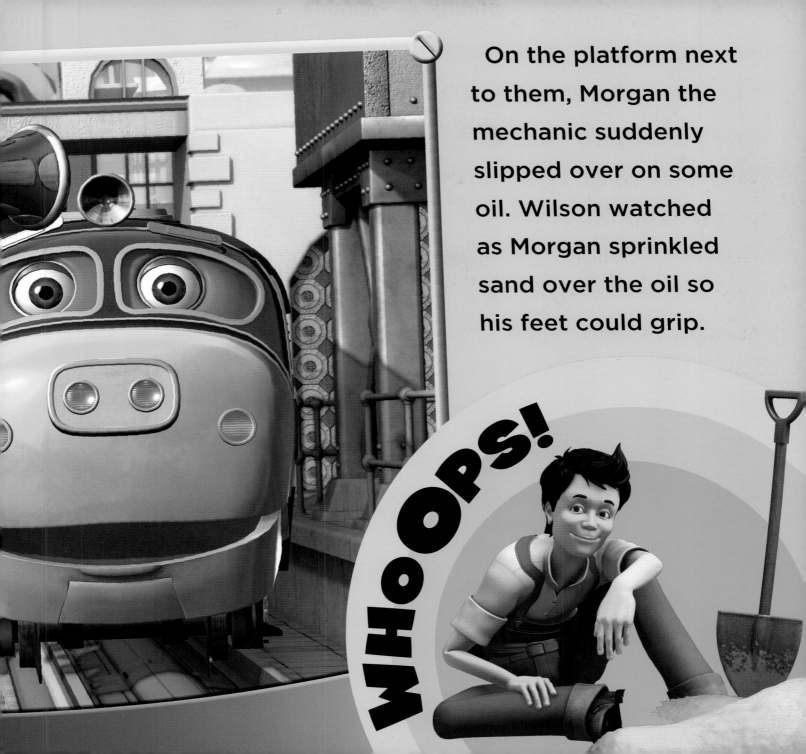

On the platform next to them, Morgan the mechanic suddenly slipped over on some oil. Wilson watched as Morgan sprinkled sand over the oil so his feet could grip.

WHOOPS!

When Brewster and Wilson came out of the tunnel and looked up at the mountain, they saw it was a very long way away.

ZOOoooOM!

They climbed the track, higher and higher up the mountain. Suddenly there were two tunnels in front of them.

Wilson couldn't remember what tunnel they had to take. He wished he'd listened more carefully to Vee, but he thought they needed the right one...

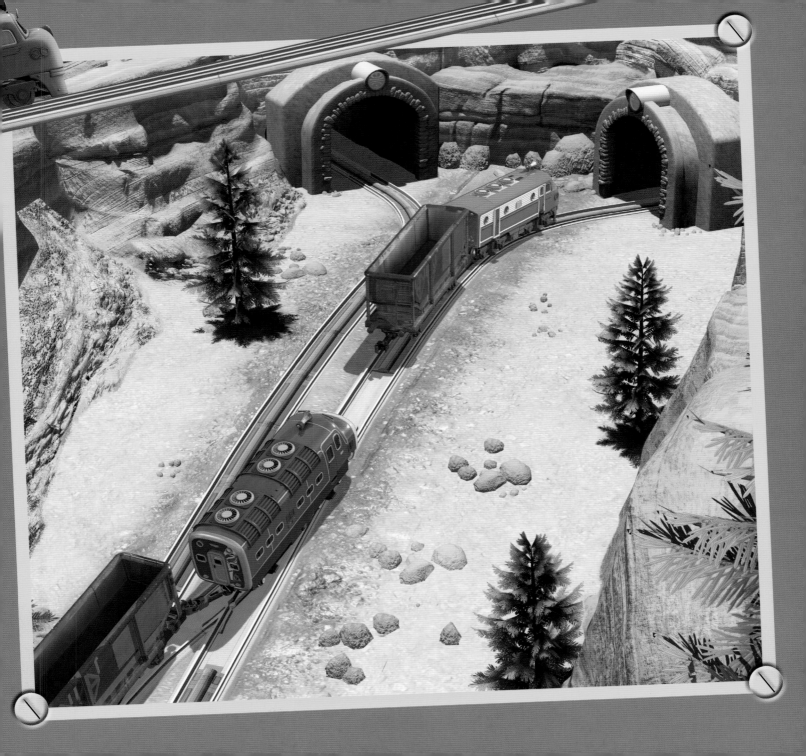

Before long, the tracks began to slope downwards "Honking horns – we're going downhill!" said Brewster, worriedly.

They were going the wrong way! After turning around, they rushed back uphill and chose the tunnel on the left this time.

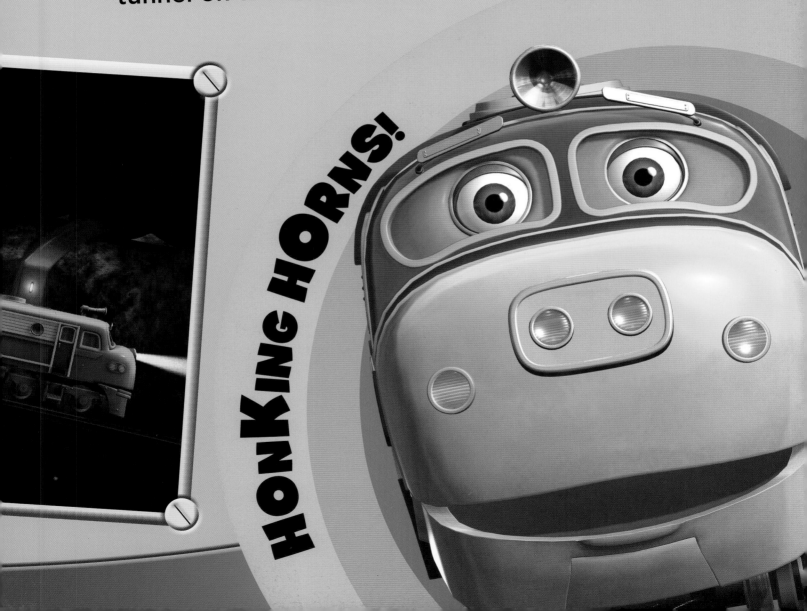

HONKING HORNS!

When they finally arrived, Karen, the quarry worker, loaded stones into Wilson's hopper car. Wilson struggled to keep his doors shut so Brewster offered to go first.

But when it was Wilson's turn, there was only dust left!

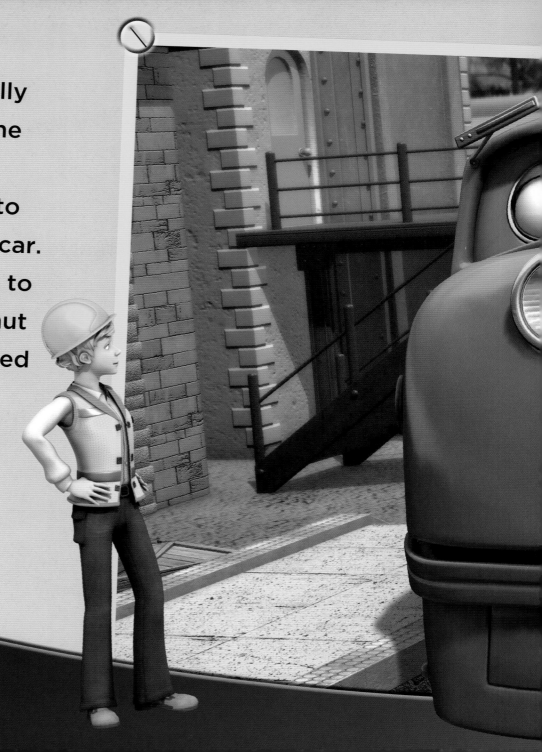

Brewster wanted to get back to the yard and zoomed ahead, but Wilson remembered Dunbar's warning – to be extra careful going downhill.

"Downhill's easy peasy," Brewster said.

Suddenly, the track became very steep and Brewster whizzed down the mountainside, out of control! "My brakes don't work. Help! I can't grip the rails!" he cried.

As Wilson caught up with Brewster, he had an idea. He whizzed ahead of Brewster and dropped his load of stone dust on the track.

"Brake on the dust!" Wilson called.

It worked!
They both slowed down
and came to a stop.
"Thanks, Wilson, you
saved me," said Brewster,
very relieved. Wilson had
remembered that Morgan used
the sand to help grip when he
slipped on the oil.

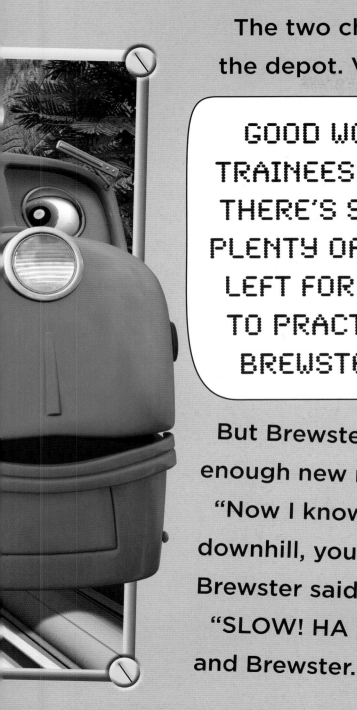

The two chuggers made their way back to the depot. Vee was pleased to see them.

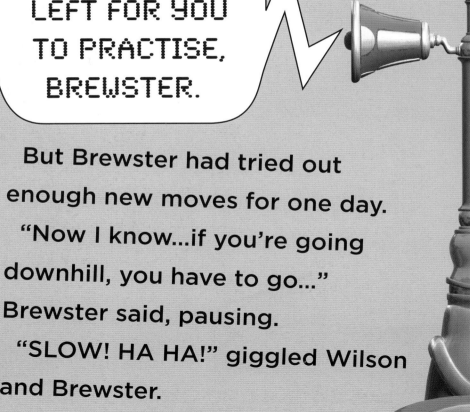

GOOD WORK, TRAINEES. AND THERE'S STILL PLENTY OF TIME LEFT FOR YOU TO PRACTISE, BREWSTER.

But Brewster had tried out enough new moves for one day. "Now I know...if you're going downhill, you have to go..." Brewster said, pausing.

"SLOW! HA HA!" giggled Wilson and Brewster.

More chuggtastic books to collect!

Complete your Chuggington collection.
Tick them off as you collect!

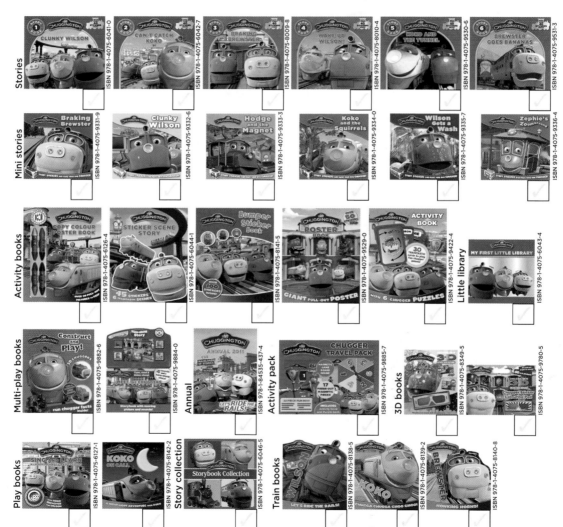

Stories

CLUNKY WILSON — ISBN 978-1-4075-6041-0
CAN'T CATCH KOKO — ISBN 978-1-4075-6042-7
BRAKING BREWSTER — ISBN 978-1-4075-8009-8
WAKE UP WILSON! — ISBN 978-1-4075-8010-4
KOKO AND THE TUNNEL — ISBN 978-1-4075-9530-6
BREWSTER GOES BANANAS — ISBN 978-1-4075-9531-3

Mini stories

Braking Brewster — ISBN 978-1-4075-9331-9
Clunky Wilson — ISBN 978-1-4075-9332-6
Hodge and the Magnet — ISBN 978-1-4075-9333-3
Koko and the Squirrels — ISBN 978-1-4075-9334-0
Wilson Gets a Wash — ISBN 978-1-4075-9335-7
Zephie's Zoom around — ISBN 978-1-4075-9336-4

Activity books

COPY COLOUR POSTER BOOK — ISBN 978-1-4075-6126-4
STICKER SCENE STORY — ISBN 978-1-4075-6044-1
Bumper Sticker Book — ISBN 978-1-4075-8141-5
POSTER BOOK — ISBN 978-1-4075-9529-0
ACTIVITY BOOK — ISBN 978-1-4075-9422-4

Little library

MY FIRST LITTLE LIBRARY — ISBN 978-1-4075-6043-4

Multi-play books

Construct and Play! — ISBN 978-1-4075-9882-6
Turn and Story — ISBN 978-1-4075-9884-0

Annual

CHUGGINGTON ANNUAL 2011 — ISBN 978-1-84535-437-4

Activity pack

CHUGGER TRAVEL PACK — ISBN 978-1-4075-9885-7

3D books

3D — ISBN 978-1-4075-8349-5
Chugger Sticker Colouring Pad — ISBN 978-1-4075-9780-5

Play books

SING AND LEARN — ISBN 978-1-4075-6127-1
KOKO ON CALL — ISBN 978-1-4075-8142-2

Story collection

Storybook Collection — ISBN 978-1-4075-6046-5

Train books

WILSON — ISBN 978-1-4075-8138-5
KOKO — ISBN 978-1-4075-8139-2
BREWSTER — ISBN 978-1-4075-8140-8